For Jake, Ben, and Isaac

Text copyright © Jonny Zucker, 2009
Illustrations copyright © Ned Woodman, 2009

"Mission 6: Short Circuit" was originally published in English in 2009. This edition is
published by an arrangement with STRIPES PUBLISHING, an imprint of Magi Publications.

Copyright © 2013 by Darby Creek

Darby Creek
A division of Lerner Publishing Group, Inc.
241 First Avenue North
Minneapolis, MN 55401 U.S.A.

Website address: www.lernerbooks.com

Library of Congress Cataloging-in-Publication Data

Zucker, Jonny.
 Short circuit / by Jonny Zucker ; illustrated by Ned Woodman.
    pages   cm. — (Max Flash ; mission 6)
 Originally published in the United Kingdom by Stripes Publishing, 2009.
 Summary: "Investigating strange signals from a warehouse, Max finds himself transported
to a parallel world inhabited entirely by futuristic robots. The sinister cyborgs are
preparing to wage war on humans using their deadly state-of-the-art new weapon. Is there
anything Max can do to stop them?"— Provided by publisher.
    ISBN 978–1–4677–1211–8 (lib. bdg. : alk. paper)
    ISBN 978–1–4677–2056–4 (eBook)
 [1. Robots—Fiction. 2. Cyborgs—Fiction. 3. Space and time—Fiction. 4. Adventure and
adventurers—Fiction.] I. Woodman, Ned, 1978– illustrator. II. Title.
    PZ7.Z77925Sh 2013
[Fic]—dc23   2012049023

Manufactured in the United States of America
1 — BP — 7/15/13

MAX FLASH
MISSION 6
SHORT CIRCUIT

Jonny Zucker

Illustrated by
Ned Woodman

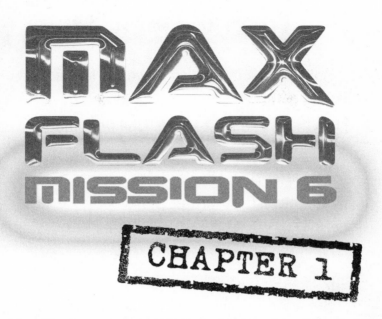

CHAPTER 1

Max Flash was trapped. Only his head and feet
stuck out from the metal box. He was blinded
by the bright lights shining from the ceiling.
His body was tensed for action. He heard the
sound of whispered voices. He twisted to the
right just as a huge steel saw sliced through
the case. The saw narrowly missed his arm.
It lodged into a slot on the opposite side and
stayed firmly in place. Max twisted again as a
second saw pierced the case. This one only just
missed his leg.

A line of sweat trickled down his forehead. He knew that timing and body position were everything in this situation. One false move and he'd be sushi.

Saw after saw followed. Max dodged them by rapid twists and turns of his body. He was twisted to the limit now. Every joint felt the strain of holding its position. One more saw and he'd be finished.

But another flash of metal didn't pierce the case. Max watched with relief as the first of the saws was whipped out of the box. The others quickly followed. Slowly he straightened his body. He pushed up with his arms, and the lid of the case sprung open. He sat up triumphantly and waved his arms in the air.

The crowd went wild. They cheered and clapped. Max acknowledged their applause and leaped down onto the stage. The audience rose to their feet. Their catcalls and shouts got louder.

His mom and dad strode across the stage to join him. Then the three of them took a bow.

The heavy stage curtain fell. Dad put an arm round Max's shoulder.

"You were brilliant," he said proudly.

"As always," added Mom.

"Don't embarrass me!" groaned Max.

"Come on," said Dad, "get changed as quickly as possible. It's a school night. Let's get you home."

Max's parents were Montgomery and Carly Flash. They were magicians. (Their stage names were The Great Montello and Mystical Cariba.) Max had been taking part in their shows for some time now. His favorite part of the show was definitely the grand finale—*The Saws of Death*.

Max was allowed to do several performances a month. He just had to keep up with his schoolwork. He loved being onstage. Keeping up with his schoolwork wasn't quite as much fun.

MAX FLASH

The audience filed out of the theater. Max's parents went to their changing room, and Max went to his. That's what he liked best about performing at the Royal Theatre in London. Here he got a room all to himself! He shut the door and sat down at his dressing table. He was busy reliving the performance in his head. He was surprised to see his reflection vanish from the mirror. A second later the cold, blue-eyed face of Zavonne appeared in its place.

"Max, I have something urgent to discuss with you," she said seriously.

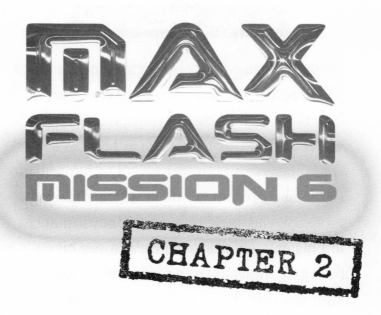

MISSION 6

CHAPTER 2

Max knew by now that he shouldn't be
surprised. Zavonne's image appeared in the
most unexpected places. But it still freaked
him out.

She can get anywhere!

Zavonne worked for an organization called
the DFEA. (That is, the Department for
Extraordinary Activity). The DFEA dealt with
strange and inexplicable events. A gang of
Zorcan Vultures from the planet Proog heads to
Earth? The DFEA cuts them off. Plague-bearing

Stone Demons emerge from the world's chalk quarries? The DFEA moves in to repel them. They dealt with all these perilous situations. And the official authorities were never even aware there was a problem.

Max had been recruited as a DFEA operative because of his incredible contortionist powers and his mastery of magic. He'd honed these skills by performing in his parents' shows. His mom and dad had carried out a couple of DFEA missions in the past too. That's how the organization had heard about Max. But that was way back. Max had now carried out *five* DFEA missions single-handed.

"The DFEA has been picking up bursts of strange magnetic waves for the last twenty-four hours," said Zavonne. "They are coming from a warehouse by the River Thames in London."

Zavonne's face vanished from the mirror. An image of a huge steel warehouse appeared.

"We staked out the building," Zavonne's voice continued over the image. "We spotted these two interesting-looking characters after one of these wave transmissions."

Max watched as two figures emerged from the warehouse. One was about six feet tall. The other was no more than four and a half feet tall.

They were both wearing motorbike gear. They had on black leather jackets and pants and heavy black biking boots. They had on crash helmets. And their faces were covered with silver ski masks. They mounted a large motorbike and sped away from the warehouse.

"A DFEA team tracked them. They watched them visiting a range of locations," said Zavonne. "At each one they stopped to take photos."

The image quickly cut to footage of the two figures posing for each other at popular tourist spots in London. First they posed on a busy shopping street. Then they posed in front of a large movie theater in Leicester Square.

Isn't Zavonne being a bit . . . paranoid?

"Surely there's nothing wrong with having your photo taken," said Max. "Even if you are wearing a ski mask. And even if you have come from a warehouse that's sending out magnetic waves."

"Agreed," said Zavonne.

"Well, maybe they're just scientists who have a lab in the warehouse and go sightseeing in their spare time."

"We used state-of-the-art DFEA imaging technology on these pictures," stated Zavonne briskly. "And these are the results."

Max stared at the screen. The two figures in their motorbike helmets and ski masks became pixelated. The image refocused. Max let out a gasp.

There staring back at him were two extremely fierce-looking *robots*.

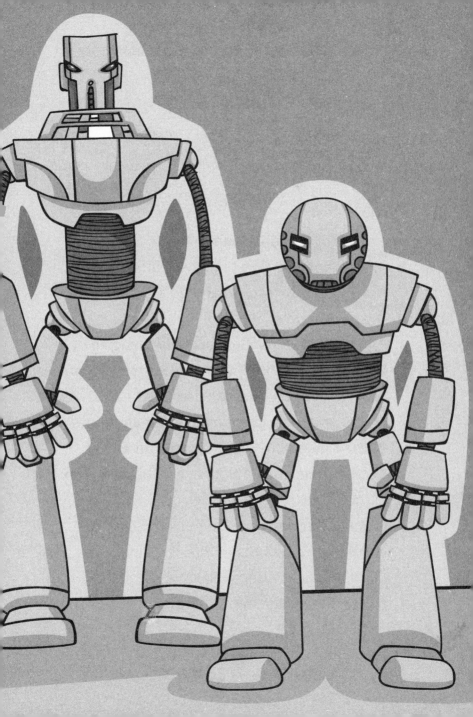

MISSION 6

CHAPTER 3

Robot tourists! Mental—or should I say metal!

The tall robot had a sleek silver rectangular head with small oval eyes and a tiny circular nose. There was a series of light and dark green digital panels fixed across his throat. The small one had a larger circular head with square eyes. He had a series of opaque dials running down either side of his chin. They looked like sideburns.

Their images disappeared. Zavonne's face reappeared in the mirror.

"These two are the most sophisticated robots the DFEA has ever come across," she informed Max. "They have made frequent visits to other locations in London. Their appearance is always preceded by a burst of magnetic waves. They then return to the warehouse, where another set of magnetic waves signals their departure. We digitally analyzed these waves. And we believe these robots are using some sort of portal that takes them to and from a parallel world."

Robotsville? Excellent!

"But there is something else," said Zavonne.

"Yes?" said Max.

"We managed to pick up fragments of their conversations. We heard them refer to something they called 'Weapon Z'."

Max shivered.

"We're convinced they've developed a new, deadly weapon. We believe they are staking out locations from which to launch their attack on our world."

"So you want me to investigate these robot guys?" asked Max.

Zavonne nodded.

"Your contortionist skills could come in very handy on a mission like this. And being smaller than an adult means you'll be far more able to disguise and hide yourself. That will probably be necessary. We want you to travel through the portal into the robot world. We want you to find out exactly what it is they're planning."

Max met Zavonne's intense gaze.

Bring it on!

"We need you to find out three things. Where are they coming from? What kind of weapon are they developing? What is the significance of the locations they've visited? This information could be crucial to the survival of the human race."

So, no pressure then!

"And you're going to give me robot-style gadgets, right?" asked Max, his eyes lighting up with anticipation.

"I will give you whatever gadgets I see fit," replied Zavonne sharply.

Sor-eee!

"There are three items inside the top drawer of your dressing table," said Zavonne.

Max pulled open the drawer and found three packages. They were labeled 1, 2, and 3.

"Open the first," commanded Zavonne.

Max placed packages 2 and 3 on the table. He opened number 1. Inside were what looked like two green squishy juggling balls.

"Those are called Suction Creepers," explained Zavonne. "They will attach themselves to any surface. A wall is a good example. They will allow the user to climb to the top. Their power lasts for sixty seconds."

Shinning up walls just like Spiderman— excellent!

"Now open the second one."

Inside was a wafer-thin mobile phone. It was flashier than any model Max had ever seen.

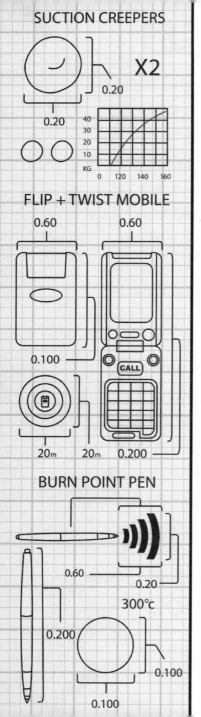

SUCTION CREEPERS

X2

0.20

0.20

40
30
20
10
KG

0　120　140　160

FLIP + TWIST MOBILE

0.60　　0.60

0.100

CALL

20m　20m　0.200

BURN POINT PEN

0.60

0.20

300°c

0.200

0.100

0.100

"That is a Flip + Twist Mobile," explained Zavonne. "Flip the phone open and press the CALL button. Then the microchip inside will undo any nuts, bolts, and screws within a twenty-meter radius."

Cool!

"The third gadget is a Burn Point Pen."

Max pulled out what looked like an ordinary red pen.

"Click the button on top, and the pen tip will produce enough heat to burn a hole in any material."

Fiendish!

"But remember, Max," cautioned Zavonne. "These gadgets may only be used in

extreme situations, or if your life is in danger."

"Yes, Zavonne," sighed Max. He'd heard this instruction a zillion times before!

"And there's just one more thing," Zavonne added. "You'll find a warp-proof suit and helmet in your wardrobe. The DFEA have developed this for all forms of interdimensional travel. That means you should be able to travel through the portal into the robots' world without any negative effects."

Just then, Zavonne's phone rang. Max watched as she picked it up. She listened in silence for a few seconds and then killed the call.

"We have just picked up a new set of magnetic waves," she said grimly. "This would seem to indicate that the robots have traveled through the portal and are with us once again. I want you to go to the warehouse immediately. A DFEA car will be here to pick you up in five minutes."

MAX FLASH MISSION 6

CHAPTER 4

Max ran to his parents' dressing room and explained the situation.

"I have to go," he said. "Zavonne's arranged for a car to pick me up outside the theater."

"I guess you'll be missing school tomorrow, then," sighed Mom. She gave him a tight hug.

"Just take care," said Dad. He squeezed Max on the shoulder. "You don't know what these robots are capable of."

"I'll be fine," Max reassured them. "Zavonne's given me some excellent gadgets and clothes."

He found the warp-proof suit and helmet hanging in his wardrobe, as promised. They were made of shiny blue material and fitted tightly to his body. Once dressed, he stuffed his gadgets in the suit's pockets.

Max hurried out of the theater. It was late, and a pale sliver of moon illuminated the dark sky. A black sedan with tinted windows was parked on the opposite curb. He crossed the road, and a door clicked open. He slid into the backseat. The DFEA driver said a quick "hello." Then he said nothing. Thirty minutes later the car pulled up outside the gates of a large industrial park.

"It's the third unit down," said the driver.

Max thanked him and got out. The driver spun the car round and sped away.

Max strode down the wide road. He walked past a printing workshop and a factory making industrial gloves. There was nobody else about.

The steel warehouse looked even bigger up

close. Its large front entrance was closed and padlocked. Max slipped round the side. He scanned the high walls for an entry point. But there was none. He hurried on to the back of the building and spotted a small air vent on top of a ledge. It was just above his head. He pulled himself up onto the ledge and quickly looked around. The whole place was dead.

Max pulled the wire mesh off the front of the vent. He squashed his arms and legs into his body and tucked his head to his chest. This let him squeeze his way, feet first, through the vent. Then he replaced the mesh behind him.

Max found himself on a ledge inside the building. He pulled out a flashlight and swung its beam across the walls. The warehouse was filled with floor-to-ceiling shelving units.

He jumped down and walked along the rows and rows of towering shelves. Every single one of them was empty.

No sign of their Weapon Z—unless of course it's invisible!

The lights flickered to life. Max heard heavy footsteps. He quickly dived behind one of the units and peered out.

About fifty meters away he saw the two robots. One was tall and sleek. The other was short and squat. Their faces gleamed with metallic menace.

"That's the last of the locations scouted, Krusher," said the shorter one. "We're now ready for the first deliveries."

"Excellent, Spike." The tall robot nodded. "Now, let us return and attend to the final preparations."

The robots came to a halt about ten meters away from Max. He watched as Krusher pressed some kind of black key fob. A metallic circular panel on the warehouse floor raised by a meter.

The portal?

The robots stepped onto the panel.

Instantly, one of the warehouse's large ceiling lights swiveled in their direction. It cast a brilliant white light on the circle. Its edges started to flash. A split second later the robots completely vanished.

The ceiling light was still focused on the circular panel. But Max could see the light starting to pulse and fade.

It's now or never!

He jumped out from his hiding place and leaped forward onto the panel.

A tingling sensation fizzed over his body. He felt himself being catapulted upward at an unbelievable speed. Max closed his eyes and clenched his fists as his stomach lurched.

Forget white-knuckle rides in theme parks— this is out of this world!

Suddenly Max came to a jolting halt.

He took a deep breath and opened his eyes.

Max was standing on a metallic circular
panel with a spotlight fixed above it. It was
identical to the one in the warehouse. He
jumped off the panel, and his eyes grew to
the size of plates as he gazed at the scene in
front of him.

The panel was set about fifteen meters
back from a huge highway. Sleek hovercars
of all different shapes, sizes, and colors were
speeding silently by on both sides. And all of
them were driven by robots.

Max gulped.

Looks like I'm the only human round here. I stick out like a seriously sore thumb!

At that moment he caught sight of Krusher and Spike. They were standing by the curb a bit further down the road.

Max crept towards them.

A sleek silver hovercar pulled up. Its doors slid open, and the robots stepped inside.

How am I going to follow them now?

Just as the car was pulling off, Max spotted a yellow driverless vehicle with an AUTO TAXI sign on its side.

Well, it's worth a try!

Max waved his hand in the air. He was surprised to see the taxi crisscross between the other vehicles and skid up to the curb.

Its doors opened, and Max quickly dived in. Inside were two steel benches facing each other.

"STATE DESTINATION!" demanded an automated voice.

"Er, follow that car!" said Max, hoping the vehicle would respond to his instruction. Luckily, it did. Its doors slid shut, and it shot off. He slunk down in his seat. He prayed that he wasn't going to be spotted by a robot in another vehicle.

A few minutes went by. Max's curiosity got the better of him. He stole a glance out of the window. Ahead was a huge four-tiered bridge carrying an assortment of gleaming vehicles. Along the side of the road giant billboards

flashed past. They said things like REFRESHER OIL—LUBRICATES JOINTS THE OTHERS CAN'T REACH and RUST-PROOF INSURANCE CORP. A flying restaurant sped by. Waiter robots zipped in and out of windows with orders.

Giant mirrored skyscrapers loomed in the distance. Each was a hundred times as tall as anything on Earth. CYBER CITY—5 MILES flashed a holographic sign on the roadside.

The taxi entered the city. Max studied the many different kinds of robots walking down

the sidewalks. The taxi came to a halt at a set of traffic lights. Max watched as a robot threw a can out of a hovercar window. Instantly, metallic hands reached up from the tarmac and swept away the rubbish. Then they retreated again as the lights changed and the cars pulled away.

Max tried to gather his thoughts.

OK, I need to get a robot disguise as quickly as possible. But where will I find one? There aren't going to be any shops selling them!

Max checked the progress of the car in front. It was pulling up against the curb. A second later its two occupants got out. Max saw Krusher and Spike striding towards a gigantic skyscraper with a silver metal fist logo on its roof. The words SPR COMMAND HQ were emblazoned above the doors.

Promising! But what does SPR stand for?

Max's taxi cut past three vehicles. It almost caused a huge pileup. Then it pulled up at the

curb behind the silver hovercar.

"DESTINATION REACHED!" announced the automated voice.

"Er, thanks," said Max, getting to his feet.

The doors remained closed.

"Er, can I get out now, please?" asked Max. He watched Krusher and Spike striding up the front steps of Command HQ.

"PAYMENT OF FARE NOT FORTHCOMING," declared the taxi.

Max groaned.

How am I going to pay the fare? I don't have any cash on me. And even if I did, it's hardly likely they'd accept human money here!

He watched anxiously as the two robots approached a massive security guard robot at the top of the steps.

"PAYMENT OF FARE NOT FORTHCOMING!" repeated the taxi.

Max looked on as the security guard dipped his head low and waved the two robots through.

They must be important.

A second later Krusher and Spike disappeared inside the building.

"PAYMENT OF FARE NOT FORTHCOMING!" said the taxi a third time.

There was only one thing for it. Max grabbed the edge of the door. He used all his strength and started to pry the door open.

"UNLAWFUL OPENING OF PASSENGER DOOR!" screamed the taxi. Its voice was slightly hysterical and high-pitched. "REFRAIN

FROM TOUCHING THE DOORS!"

But Max ignored the warning. He forced the door open a fraction. Then he squashed his body through the gap and tumbled out onto the street. He ducked down behind a large silvery plant with sharp, spiked branches. Luckily, the security guard seemed not to have spotted him.

He was racking his brains for a way to get inside Command HQ without being seen when the taxi started bellowing a phrase over and over. "FARE EVADER ON THE LOOSE! FARE EVADER ON THE LOOSE! FARE EVADER ON THE LOOSE!"

CHAPTER 6

A few seconds later Max heard the stomping of metal feet. He peered out and saw a huge robot. It had silver eyes and a blue light on its head. Some kind of laser gun in a holster hung at its side. And it was pounding down the pavement in his direction.

A law enforcement official! Just what I DON'T want at the minute!

Max didn't hesitate. He dipped down an alley at the side of Command HQ. He could hear the stomping police robot behind him as

he ran to the end of the street. He took a left, then a right, then another left. He reached a junction and set off down a narrow alley on his left.

He sprinted down the gloomy alley lined with trash bins. It was a dead end.

Max heard the clunking footsteps of the police robot fast approaching. He quickly ducked behind one of the bins.

Bit smelly here. But it's better than being caught, I guess!

Max froze to the spot. The robot marched down the alley. Max felt something scuttle over his foot. He looked down slowly and saw what looked like a grubby computer mouse scuttle past.

I hope it doesn't byte!

Max listened as the robot's footsteps retreated into the distance. He waited a few more minutes until he was sure that the coast was clear and stood up. But just then a small white robot appeared round the corner. It was about Max's size. It had an orange light on its domed head. It was sweeping up rubbish with a large metal broom.

"Greetings," it said in a squeaky voice.

"Please state your task."

Max didn't think twice. He leaped onto the robot and dragged it behind the bins.

The police robot appeared at the entrance to the alley a minute later. It stopped when it noticed a small robot sweeping up rubbish.

"Hey you!" it called. "Have you seen anyone running this way? I'm looking for a fare evader."

"No one identified," squeaked the robot.

"Something wrong with your voice box?" asked the police robot with a frown.

"No," replied the robot shakily, "just got a little cold."

"A cold what?" asked the police robot. But at that moment its walkie-talkie went. It looked suspiciously at the small robot. But then it turned and marched back the way it had come.

Max breathed a heavy sigh of relief from inside the shell of the robot. His rapidly put-together disguise seemed to have worked. Luckily, the small robot hadn't put up much of a fight when Max had pounced on it. He'd had just enough time. He had hit its SHUT DOWN button, ripped open a large panel on its back, and dived inside its shell. Then he'd hastily pulled the panel closed behind him.

The suit felt clunky and uncomfortable. But it was definitely better than being exposed as a human. There was a ventilation strip in the head that he could see through. Max knew he needed to blend in, so he spent several minutes practicing walking and using his new robotic arms and hands. Max also worked on his new voice. He tried hard to emulate the squeaky tones of his victim. When he was reasonably happy with this impersonation, he set out to find Krusher and Spike.

But there was one small problem.

He had taken a lot of twists and turns. And now he had no idea how to get back to Command HQ. He didn't want to ask another robot for directions, at least not just yet. He

tried to retrace his steps and found himself on a wide, bustling street. Robots were everywhere he looked. Street vendors were selling steel burgers with microchips. Some robot children were throwing electrified glow-balls at each other that gave off an electric shock if they made contact with anything.

Max walked slowly. He tried to figure out the way back to Command HQ. But there was no sign of it. He was considering his next move when he spotted a large, low-slung building that bore the metal fist logo. It was the same logo he'd seen on the roof of Command HQ.

OK, this might not be my primary target. But there may well be something interesting inside that's connected to Command HQ and the robots' plans.

At once he began clunking towards the building.

CHAPTER 7

Max approached the building. He saw a sign stating ALL VISITORS REPORT TO RECEPTION.

What reason can I give for being here? Announcing I'm a human spy might not go down too well!

He took in his surroundings. He saw a pile of brown packages stacked on the side of a loading bay. He hurried over and made sure no one was around. Then he scooped up one of the packages and headed to Reception.

Reception turned out to be a small room

with bright-yellow walls. Max could see a robot secretary inputting some data on a tiny laptop at a glass desk.

Max cleared his throat and rapped one of his robot fingers on the glass desk.

"Yes?" the secretary asked.

"I have a delivery," announced Max in his best robot voice. He held up the brown package.

"Department?"

"Excuse me?" said Max.

The robot rolled her eyes. "Which D-e-p-a-r-t-m-e-n-t is it for?" she asked in her most patronizing speaking-to-a-toddler voice.

Max thought quickly. He didn't know what went on inside this building, let alone what the departments were called.

"It's for the Department Department," Max said without thinking.

The secretary stared at him. "Never heard of it," she replied, folding her arms.

MAX FLASH

"That's because it's only just been set up," he responded. "Things are getting more departmentalized. The various departments decided they needed a new department. It's called the Department Department for, you know, departmental things."

"Really?" the secretary said. She glared suspiciously.

"Well, it's been set up by Command HQ," said Max in desperation.

At the mention of Command HQ, however, her tone of voice changed.

"I've heard of it!" she said quickly. "I was just checking that you were a legitimate delivery robot."

"Of course I'm legitimate," said Max sharply. "Now can I please go through and drop off this vital package? The Department Department requested I deliver it personally."

She nodded. Then she leaned forward and stuck a square magnet stating VISITOR on his chest. She flicked a switch. A door to Max's right swung open. He gave her a friendly wave and headed through.

The door led to a wide passage lit by bright white spotlights. Max passed several doors on each side. Signs read "Iron Research and Development" and "Advanced Screwdriver Team". He turned right at the end of the passage and followed a flight of steps upward. This took him to another corridor. At the

end was a set of double doors with a sign.
It said, TOP SECRET. ENTRY RESTRICTED TO
AUTHORIZED PERSONNEL ONLY.

*Looks like as good a place as any to start
searching.*

Max checked that no one was around. Then
he pushed open the doors and went through. He
found himself stepping onto a narrow walkway.
The walkway stretched high above a factory floor.

It was very hot. Max immediately started to
sweat inside his robot suit. But at least the
place seemed empty.

At the end of the room was a roaring furnace. Molten metal streamed out like lava from a volcano every few seconds. It flowed into a series of molds.

The molds then snaked along a conveyer belt through a clear tunnel. Inside, hundreds of metal hands assembled the pieces. Max could just make out the finished silver objects from where he was standing. They emerged from the tunnel and dropped off the end of the conveyer belt into crates. Each one was stamped with a large letter Z.

This must be where Weapon Z is being made! But what is it? Some sort of gun?

Max headed across the walkway. He leaned over the rail to try to get a closer look at the objects. He didn't spot the large metal hand extending from the ceiling to pick up the crates.

The hand only brushed against him. But this was enough to knock Max over the rail. He landed on the conveyer belt with a crashing of metal joints. He scrambled to get up. But one of his robotic legs got caught under the conveyer belt.

Frantically, he pulled at his robot leg. But it was totally stuck.

Just ahead was a large red lever. Max reached out with one hand and managed to slam it backward. He gave a sigh of relief as the conveyer belt shuddered for a moment and seemed to come to a stop. But suddenly the belt started to move again—this time in reverse. He was heading straight for the furnace!

MISSION 6

CHAPTER 8

Max tried to wriggle out of his metal suit, but
he couldn't reach the panel on the back. By
now the furnace was only about fifteen meters
away. With each passing second he felt the
baking heat increase.

Max grimaced.

I'm facing total meltdown!

The sweat poured off his face as the blasting
furnace loomed ever nearer.

Ten meters to go. I'll be fried for sure.

Suddenly Max remembered the Burn

Point Pen. Twisting from side to side, he dislodged the pen from his pocket. By bending backwards, he tilted it toward his head. He gave a sharp nod and jerked the pen out through the helmet's ventilation strip.

The heat was almost unbearable now. Max gripped the pen in his hand, stretched out, and drew a line across the belt in front of him. Smoke trailed from the pen's nib.

The conveyer belt glowed red, then buckled. It flung Max through the air. He landed on the floor with a thud and lay there, panting.

Phew! That was a lucky escape!

Max slowly got to his feet. He was just about to check out the weapons when a shrill alarm sounded. "MACHINERY MALFUNCTION," screeched a robotic voice.

Not again!

Max heard the sound of running footsteps. He quickly stumbled over toward a door marked EXIT and pushed his way through. He found himself back on the main street.

OK, I didn't see what the weapons are, but I now know the robots are definitely making something. I need to get inside Command HQ and find out some more info!

This time the street was even more packed than before. Max found himself caught up in a crowd of robots. Some were carrying banners and others shaking rattles.

Max was swept along by the crowd. He heard the sound of chanting and clapping. In front of him towered a giant stadium with the words CYBER CITY in glowing green letters.

Shame I haven't got time to check out a major robot sporting event!

But a second later, Max spotted Krusher and Spike. They were being driven in their sleek silver hovercar towards the gates of the stadium. The crowds parted to let them through. The car swept past a line of staff and straight into the stadium.

If they were here to watch a game, Max was going to watch it too!

He joined the crowd and walked under a large arch into the stadium. Ahead of him was a great throng of robots. Some were drinking frothing grey liquid from large tankards. Others were heading straight to their seats.

But there was one problem. To reach the inside of the stadium you had to pass through

one of fifty automated ticket entrances. And Max had no ticket. No ticket meant no game. No game meant losing Krusher and Spike again.

I MUST get in!

Max watched the crowds for a few moments. Eventually he spotted a family of five trying to make their way through one of the barriers. Their smallest child was a small mauve-and-white robot with goofy, jagged teeth. He had sneaked back through the entrance, which then closed again, denying him access. One of the ushers beckoned the family to come to an entrance at the far end. The usher had a key for this and held the gate open.

Max saw his chance. He hurried towards the gate. He nipped ahead of the robot child and passed through.

"Oy! Stop!" shouted the usher. But Max was already lost in the crowd.

Woo-hoo! I've made it!

Max looked around. He saw Krusher and

Spike climbing some steps that led to Block 4. He hurried after them and found himself inside the arena.

Banks upon banks of seats looked out over the bright-green rubber pitch. A massive screen stood at each corner of the stadium to provide replays and clips of legendary games.

Max hurried down the stairs. He spotted a free seat just behind Krusher and Spike, six rows from the front.

I never get seats this good when I go to soccer matches back home!

Max sat down and tried to listen in on their conversation over the chatter of the crowd.

"Are you sure we should be here, Krusher?" said Spike, the smaller robot.

"I'm not missing this match for anything!" snapped Krusher. "Anyway, this is as good a place as any to pick up some recruits to help us with the final stages of our Great Plan."

Great Plan?

Max leaned forward to try to hear more. But just as he did so, a gigantic purple robot in the seat behind stood up and loomed over him.

"What do you think YOU'RE doing here?" it demanded, pointing an accusing metal finger.

CHAPTER 9

Max gulped nervously. He looked around wildly for an escape route.

Has my back panel come off? Does he know I'm a human in disguise?

The robot grabbed him by the shoulder and pulled him to his feet.

"Tier 96 is your section," it told him crossly. "That's where you need to be."

Max almost asked why he belonged in Tier 96, but he didn't want to draw any more attention to himself. He edged past the other

supporters. He spotted Tier 96 right at the top of Block 4. He hurried up the steps. He noticed that all the robots sitting there were identical to him. They had the same white shells and orange lights on the top of their dome-shaped heads.

Maybe we're the away supporters?

Max squeezed past three robots and placed himself on an empty seat.

"It's great going to other teams' stadiums, isn't it?" he said to the robot on his left, testing out this theory. "You know—being an away supporter?"

The robot swiveled round and fixed him with a weird look. "This is the home section," it said sharply. "If you want the away section, it's in Block 25."

"Of course!" Max nodded quickly. "I was only joking. I'm the world's biggest Cyber City fan!"

The crowd suddenly roared as the two teams came out onto the field. Each one had ten players. They were all massive and all shaking their fists at each other.

"Who are we playing again?" said Max to the robot beside him.

"Bolt United," replied the robot sharply.

Max looked at the pitch and noticed there wasn't a ball anywhere in sight. A buzzer sounded. Max immediately saw the reason for the lack of a ball. It seemed that the object of the game was for the robot players to attack each other. The crashing of metal against metal rang through the stadium. And the roar of the crowd accompanied each and every collision. The details of the match were continually updated on the jumbo screens.

DIRECT BELLY HITS: UNITED 7 - CITY 3

HEAD-ON COLLISIONS: UNITED 4 - CITY 4

BUTT KICKS: UNITED 6 - CITY 2

Max kept looking out for Krusher and Spike. But he found himself being swept up in the action. Soon he was cheering and shouting like all of the other robots in Tier 96.

He didn't spot Krusher and Spike rapidly climbing up the steps towards Tier 96. He didn't see them pointing toward him and his neighbors.

A split second later, Max felt a jolt as the bottom of his seat dropped away and he found himself falling into blackness.

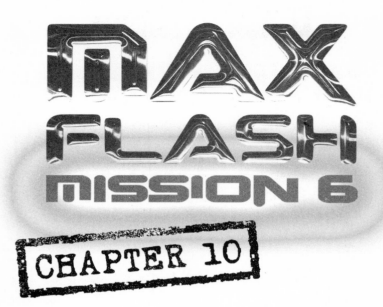

MISSION 6

CHAPTER 10

As Max's eyes got used to the gloom, he saw
he was plummeting toward a large open-top
truck. He landed in a crumpled heap. Moments
later his fellow supporters from the stadium
tumbled down on top of him.

As he untangled himself from the others,
Max noticed that in front of him stood a neat
row of identical robots.

"OK, let's get moving!" he heard a voice shout
from outside, and the truck's roof slid shut.

Max cursed himself.

Why wasn't I more careful? I need to get to Command HQ. And now I'm trapped! Did Krusher and Spike see through my disguise? But if so, what are these other robots from the stadium doing here?

Some of the robots were whispering to each other about the match and the greatness of Cyber City. Max looked gloomily at the robot facing him.

"What's going on?" he asked.

The robot frowned at him. "Same as usual," it replied.

"The usual being?"

"We were allowed out for the day to watch the match, but we've been recalled before the end."

"What have we been let out of?" asked Max.

"Are you in denial?" asked the robot with suspicion. "We're drones, *remember*? We serve wherever we're directed. That's what comes with being in the lowest level of society."

Drones? The lowest level of society?

Max could have hit himself. That was why he'd been directed to Tier 96 in the stadium. It was reserved for drones—the lowest of the low!

Why couldn't I have stolen the shell of a robot VIP?

"But look on the bright side," said another drone. "This isn't any old job we've been recalled for. This is the Big One!"

"What's that?" asked Max.

"We're about to find out!" replied the drone eagerly.

Max groaned. *That's helpful! What a nightmare! Now I'll never get near Command HQ. And the robots will unleash their terrifying weapon on humans . . . whatever it is!*

Suddenly the drone opposite Max shouted, "Is everyone up for this?"

The answers came quickly.

"Totally!"

"Wicked!"

"Right on!"

They were all brimming with excitement. Max shook his head in disbelief.

These guys are actually looking forward to being servants!

After another few minutes the vehicle pulled to a halt. The back doors of the truck opened. Max and the other drones streamed out into a large, airy room and formed a neat line.

"Drones!" called out a powerful and throaty voice from somewhere.

The drones bowed their heads low.

A second later, Krusher and Spike stepped into the room. They were followed by a mean-looking robodog, which started snapping at the heels of the drones. A trail of oily goo dripped from its steel jaws.

"Heel, Metal Meathead!" commanded Spike. The dog obediently stopped attacking the drones' feet and ran over to his master's side.

Metal Meathead? That doesn't sound like a gentle pet!

"Welcome, drones!" declared Krusher. "Welcome to Command HQ!"

MISSION 6

CHAPTER 11

Command HQ?

Max couldn't believe his metal ears. Finally he'd made it. Yes, he was here as a servant. But at least he'd get a chance to look for clues about what was going on.

Being a drone has got me just where I want to be!

"Right," declared Krusher. "I have important business to deal with, so Spike will show you to your task. The time for the Great Plan is nearly upon us!" With that, Krusher turned and disappeared somewhere inside the building.

What IS the Great Plan? If I don't find out soon, my mission will be a total wipeout!

"Now listen up, drones!" said Spike sharply. "You are to carry out this task with the utmost drone diligence."

"Yes, Master Spike," chirped the drones. "We will carry it out with the utmost drone diligence!"

"And bear this in mind," hissed Spike menacingly. "Metal Meathead here doesn't take kindly to shirkers, gossipers, or robots with a bad attitude. Understand?"

"Yes, Master Spike," responded the drones.

"You are to prepare the delivery trucks. They must be emptied out and made spick-and-span!"

"Most definitely, Master Spike!" trilled the drones.

He clapped his hands, and the drones followed Spike. Max hurried to keep up. Metal Meathead brought up the rear.

They marched through a large door and down some steps into a wide courtyard at the back of the building.

Ahead sat a line of trucks. Spike quickly split the drones up into pairs.

"Right," he said, "begin your clear out. I'm leaving Metal Meathead here to keep an eye on you."

And with that Spike headed back into the building.

"I'm Max," whispered Max to the drone he had been paired with. "What's your name?"

"I'm Snap," the drone replied, looking slightly confused. "Now let's get started," he added earnestly.

They walked round to the back of their first truck. Slowly they began to clear out the junk from inside—mostly rusty old tools and damaged computer terminals.

"What's going to go in these trucks?" Max asked Snap.

"Our job is to do, not to question," answered Snap.

"But you must know something?"

"Our brains only store data relevant to our immediate tasks," replied Snap.

Max sighed. If he couldn't pry anything out of Snap, he'd just have to start searching for himself. He glanced toward the building. Metal Meathead was standing directly in front of the door. He was drooling and keeping his beady eyes fixed on the drones.

I don't fancy a run-in with Meathead! I need to find something that will keep a robodog occupied.

Max hunted through the truck and pulled out a rusty wrench.

Suppose this will have to do . . .

"Hey, Snap," he called, "I'm going to take a short break."

Snap gazed at him blankly. "What's a break?"

"It's a . . . don't worry about it," Max said. "My joints just need a bit of a stretch."

"An unauthorized move, how irregular," said Snap, puzzled. "Well, don't be long."

"I won't," replied Max, walking toward the building. When he was about twenty meters away from Metal Meathead, he threw the wrench through the air to the far side of the courtyard.

"Fetch!"

The robodog watched it spin through the air and immediately gave chase.

Max ran toward the door, hoping the bait had bought him enough time. But just as he was reaching out for the handle, he heard a bloodcurdling growl from behind.

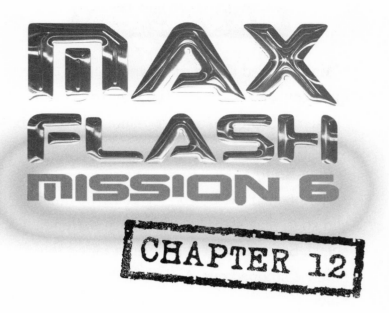

Max watched in horror as Metal Meathead
leaped through the air at him. He yanked the
door open as hard as he could. It smashed into
the dog and propelled Max backwards.

Max dived through the door. He pulled
it firmly shut behind him. He heard Metal
Meathead run at the door and start pawing
at it. He was yelping in frustration.

That was close!

His heart was racing. Max crept down the
corridor. To his right was a glass elevator.

Max stepped inside. He scanned the gleaming silver buttons. They ran from "Basement: Drone Zone" to "Floor 101: Control Center."

Interesting . . .

He touched the button for 101. The doors slid shut. Max was shot upward at extreme speed. Seconds later the elevator jolted to a halt. He stepped out. And walked straight into Spike.

"What are YOU doing here?"

Spike was carrying a large, wafer-thin TV.

"Just meeting with the packing team," blurted out Max. He tried to use to his best drone voice. "I must have got the wrong floor."

"Meeting!" cried Spike. "You're a drone! Your job is not to meet! Who sent you here?"

"Krusher!" blurted out Max.

Spike sighed. "OK, make yourself useful. Take this screen to the Viewing Room on your

way down. You need to hang it on the wall. Think you can manage that? The room's on floor 26. Make sure you get the right place this time."

He handed Max the TV screen. The screen was heavier than it looked. Max staggered backward.

"Well, get a move on!" shouted Spike. He pushed Max back into the elevator.

I need to check out that Control Center. But there's no chance with Spike around. I'll drop off the screen. Hopefully he'll be gone by the time I return.

As the elevator descended, Max heard a loud announcement on a loud speaker.

"ALL DRONES REPORT TO THE VIEWING ROOM IMMEDIATELY! ALL DRONES REPORT TO THE VIEWING ROOM IMMEDIATELY!"

Max got out of the elevator on floor 26. A few moments later he saw a whole line of drones marching toward a blue door. He

followed them inside. He spotted a cable
sticking out of the wall. Max lifted the screen
onto his shoulder. He climbed up onto a small
stepladder and connected the screen.

More and more drones were arriving. Within
minutes the room was full. They stood in neat
lines awaiting the start of the broadcast. Max
joined the back row. He found himself next
to Snap.

The letters SPR filled the screen.

"What's that?" Max whispered.

"The Society for the Protection of Robots, of course," answered Snap. "You must know that!"

"Greetings, drones," said a presenter's voice. "And welcome to your final instruction broadcast. We know you have far below average robot intelligence. But even you should get the gist of what's about to follow."

Max looked around at the drones. Their faces were glued to the screen.

"In thirty minutes the final stage of our Great Plan will be put into action. We will travel to The Other Side as conquerors!"

There was a cheer from the collected drones.

Max gulped. *Conquerors!*

"We must never forget the reason for this quest," said the voice.

The screen filled with pictures of humans constructing robots on assembly lines. Then the humans were putting the robots inside cars that were smashed against walls. The next images showed children with toy robots. The children flung them around and even pulled off the robots' limbs.

The drones booed at the images on the screen.

"That is how they treat us!" snarled the presenter's voice. "So revenge will be sweet!"

The drones cheered and gave each other high fives.

OK, thought Max. *They believe that humans mistreat them. So they want to get their own back using their Weapon Z to conquer Earth. But I need to find out exactly what this is— and fast!*

Max turned. He started tiptoeing toward the door. All of the drones were still staring up at the screen.

All except one.

"Hey, where are you going? We've been

instructed to watch the entire program."

Max spun round.

It was Snap.

"I've been assigned to another task," said Max. He edged toward the door.

"Really?" asked Snap. "What kind of task?"

"I'd love to tell you," whispered Max. "But it's top secret."

"But drones' work is never top secret," pointed out Snap. He raised his voice. "One unauthorized move is bad. BUT TWO IS UNACCEPTABLE!"

The other drones turned round to see what was going on. Max was right by the door now. Snap stepped forward and blocked his way. A split second later, the drones all started moving in on him.

MISSION 6

CHAPTER 13

As the drones surrounded Max they started chanting.

"Our aim is to serve!"

"Obey and follow!"

"Respond to orders!"

"No unauthorized moves!"

"They think, drones do!"

"I'm not your average drone," replied Max coolly. He rammed into the nearest drone, who toppled into the others.

Max sprinted across the room. He climbed

up onto the stepladder. The drones got to
their feet and chased after him. Soon he was
surrounded again. But this was exactly what
Max wanted. Max grabbed the TV screen
from the wall. He launched himself off the
stepladder. He used the drones' domed heads
as stepping-stones back toward the exit.

Max dived off the last drone's head. He sailed
through the doorway. He slammed the door and
used the screen to jam it shut behind him. Then
he raced off down the corridor.

He reached the elevator and slammed the button for floor 101.

Time to check out that Control Center!

Max stepped out of the elevator. As he reached the large metal door to the Control Center, he could hear voices from inside. It was Krusher and Spike.

Max crouched down. He peered through the keyhole.

"So you have the complete list of places?" Krusher was asking.

"Yes," replied Spike.

"Once we have all of our foot soldiers in place, I will be able to control their every move with this Activation Pod!" Krusher pulled out a shiny black object shaped like an egg. On the top was a gleaming silver button.

"I can't wait for tonight's big show in the square." Krusher laughed.

The square? Does he mean another portal? A square portal, not a round one this time?

Suddenly Max saw Metal Meathead running toward the door.

Yikes!

He ducked down.

Metal Meathead started pawing at the door.

"What is it, Meathead?" demanded Spike. He walked over to the door.

Max turned and fled. Luckily, the room next door was unlocked. He dived inside. It appeared to be some kind of research lab. He listened as the door to the Control Center clicked open.

The moment Meathead was released he caught Max's scent. Meathead bounded over to the lab door, barking furiously.

"There's something in there," said Spike. He reached out for the door handle.

"LEAVE IT!" ordered Krusher. "We need to get going. Time is of the essence."

Max heard the sound of the Control Center door being locked. Then he heard Metal Meathead howl as he was dragged down the corridor.

Max waited to make sure the coast was clear. He reached his arm down inside his robot suit. He fumbled through his pockets to find something to use to unlock the door.

Chewing gum wrapper . . . no. Piece of string . . . not really. Used tissue . . . I don't think so!

Just then, he spotted an air vent on the wall. He climbed up onto one of the lab benches to investigate.

Through the vent Max had a perfect view of the Control Center.

The walls of the room were lined with giant computer screens. A map of London was covered in hundreds of large red dots. On

the next screen he could just make out a list
of words: Andertons, Kethwicks, Cooper and
Gates."

Andertons?

The name rang a bell for Max. But he
couldn't quite think where he'd heard it before.

In the center of the room was a glass table.
On this table Max spotted a shiny black egg-
shaped object with a gleaming silver button on
top.

*The Activation Pod! I've got to get my
hands on that!*

Max pulled off the grate of the air vent. He
scrambled up the wall. In the robot suit it
was a tight squeeze to get through. He just
made it. Then he fell to the floor with a loud
CLANG!

He was just about to reach for the
Activation Pod when the door was flung open.
Spike marched in. He stared in surprise at
the drone.

"How did you get in here?" demanded Spike. He snatched up the Activation Pod.

"I was directed here by Krusher," replied Max.

"Krusher would *never* authorize a drone to be in this section of the building," snapped Spike.

Max realized this trick wasn't going to work on Spike a second time. He opted for another strategy.

"Salad, dustbin, fish and chips," he blurted out.

"What did you say?" asked an incredulous looking Spike.

"Shopping, nostrils, soup," added Max. He bashed into a chair. Then he reversed and crashed into it again.

Spike shook his head. He pulled out a mobile phone.

Max spun round a couple of times. He started chanting nursery rhymes.

"Itsy bitsy spider . . ."

"I have a damaged drone over at Command HQ," Spike snarled into the phone. "I need D-Squad here now."

He listened for a few seconds.

"Yes, yes," he said impatiently, casting a quick glance at Max. "Just make sure you bring the right vehicle for drone disposal!"

MAX FLASH MISSION 6

CHAPTER 14

Max gulped. *That doesn't sound good!*

"Hurry up!" ordered Spike. He pushed Max out of the Control Center and into a service elevator. The elevator shot down, and Max found himself back in the courtyard.

The trucks from before were ready. Max watched as drones climbed into the cabs and powered up the engines. The main gates swung open. One by one the trucks pulled away.

Then he heard the roar of a very large

engine. A huge orange truck snaked around the corner and pulled into the courtyard. Three massive oval-headed robots climbed out. They had the words D-SQUAD sprayed across their chests in orange letters.

"At last," said Spike. He shoved Max in the direction of the robots. "Deal with this damaged drone at once!"

With that, Spike hurried back inside the building. The largest of the D-Squad robots bent down. He stuck his face in Max's. "So what have we got here, then? A drone that doesn't do exactly what its master tells it to?"

"Actually, I'm not damaged at all," said Max, quickly. "There's . . . there's been a mix-up with another drone. It's inside the building. I can show it to you."

Max spun round. He began marching back toward the building. But a metal arm grabbed him by the neck and pulled him back.

"We're not buying that one, are we, lads?" the huge robot chuckled.

"No way!" chorused the other two.

"You see, you're going to treat us to a spectacular show," explained the first robot. "The crunching of metal, the grinding of joints. We wouldn't miss it for the world. We like to see drones going in whole and coming out like crushed cans!"

"Call it recycling!" snickered one of the other robots.

"But you've got it wrong!" shouted Max. "I work perfectly. Go on, give me an instruction."

But D-Squad weren't having any of it. The largest robot picked up Max. The robot slung Max over his shoulder and marched to the back of the truck. Max's eyes nearly popped out of their sockets when he saw the gleaming metal teeth.

"Rev her up!" shouted the robot. The other two hopped into the cab. The engine roared.

The terrifying teeth came to life, chomping up and down with swift crunching motions.

"In you go!" laughed the big robot. "We'll see you on the other side!"

He lifted Max high into the air and prepared to feed him to the huge, gnashing teeth.

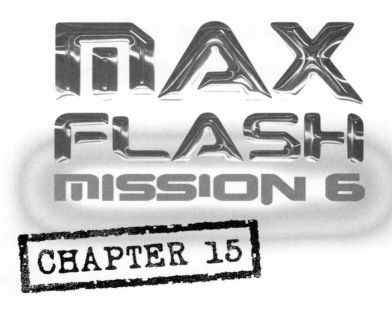

MISSION 6

CHAPTER 15

If ever there was a time for the Flip + Twist
Mobile, it was now. A split second before Max
was fed to the hungry D-Squad truck's teeth,
he whipped out the phone from his pocket.
He flipped it open and pressed the CALL
button. In an instant every single nut and bolt
within a twenty-meter radius came undone. It
was chaos!

The three D-Squad robots fell apart. The
D-Squad truck collapsed in a metallic heap.
The main gates toppled over.

And Max's robot shell fell to bits around him.

Ooops! That wasn't supposed to happen.

He'd saved himself from the jaws of the vicious truck. But now Max was fully exposed as a human. He wouldn't last for long around here if he was spotted.

Max jumped over the collapsed gates. He sprinted down the side of the building and emerged on the main street. He caught sight of Krusher, Spike, and Metal Meathead climbing into their silver car. There was no way he was going to go for the fare-evader option again. So there was only one thing for it. He raced toward the car. In one massive leap, he threw himself onto the roof just as it started to pull away.

"HEY!" shouted a robot couple in the street. They stared at the human in astonishment.

But they were too late to do anything. The car was already racing through the traffic. Max lay flat on the roof and held on tight.

The car sped down the street. It cut up other vehicles. As it approached its destination, Max recognized the large circular metal panel of the portal. But this time the light's beam was much broader and stronger than before. Max watched as a line of silver Command HQ trucks drove into the glow. They disappeared one by one.

The car pulled up, and Krusher, Spike, and Metal Meathead got out. They headed straight for the portal. Max slid off the roof. He watched as they stepped into the light.

The beam began to fade. Max had just enough time to run up and dive through.

He felt the same tingling sensation as before. His stomach flipped over. Moments later he

found himself back in the warehouse in his own world . . . lying at the feet of Krusher.

Krusher lunged forward. He dragged Max up by the scruff of his neck.

"So what have we here? A human spy?"

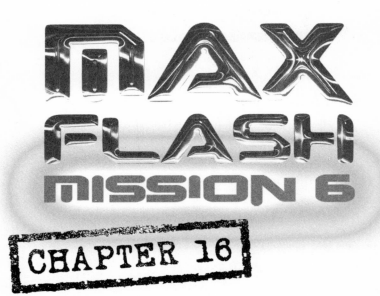

CHAPTER 16

"How did you enter our world, you repulsive human?" demanded Krusher with a terrifying snarl.

"I work for a human—robot travel agency," replied Max. He gulped as Spike and Metal Meathead moved menacingly toward him. "We need to update our brochures. So I thought I'd just pay you guys a visit and—"

"SILENCE!" barked Krusher.

Max looked around the warehouse. Before the shelves had been empty. Now they were

crammed full of steel crates. Each crate was stamped with the letter *Z*.

All the time I've been in the robot world they must have been shipping their weapons here!

A team of drones was loading the crates from the shelves into the back of the large silver trucks.

"TIME FOR YOU LOT TO HIT THE ROAD!" Krusher ordered as he dragged Max across the room.

Instantly the drones started pulling down the steel shutters on the backs of the trucks. They climbed inside. They twisted the ignition keys and gunned their engines. There was a loud buzz as the warehouse gates opened. A moment later the trucks started pouring out.

"OVER HERE, SPIKE!" shouted Krusher. "And bring me a crate."

Spike struggled over with one of the crates. Krusher turned his attentions back to Max.

"So you wish to ruin our Great Plan, do you?"

"OK," said Max, "the tourist thing was a lie. I'm . . . I'm . . . really a health and safety officer. I'm . . . I'm doing a check on all metallic dogs. You need a special license to have one."

"Do you think I was born yesterday?" Krusher snarled furiously.

"I don't know," replied Max. "Were you?"

"You INSOLENT human!" Krusher shouted. "You are a SPY, and spies must be dealt with." He turned to Spike. "Open that crate!" he ordered.

Max took a deep breath.

This is it! The moment I've been waiting for! I'm finally going to get to see the terrifying weapon they've created! I just hope they're not about to try it out on me.

Max watched intently as Spike slid the top panel of the crate open.

Is it a bomb? Is it a laser gun?

Spike reached into the box and lifted something out.

But it wasn't a gun or a bomb or anything remotely like a weapon.

It was a model robot. It had large silver eyes and a shiny blue chrome body covered in high-tech circuitry. It stood around ten centimeters tall.

Max couldn't believe his eyes. He burst out laughing. "That's it? That's your incredible new weapon to attack the human race—a crummy little toy?"

CHAPTER 17

Krusher shot Max a furious look. "You want to
see how crummy it is?" he screamed. "Let me
show you!" He tore off the packaging.

Max stopped laughing.

Maybe it wasn't so funny after all.

"Er, how does it work?" asked Max, staring
at the toy. "Is it some kind of bomb?"

"Oh, human fool!" hissed Krusher, leaning
in towards Max. "Do you really think we'd be
able to achieve our aims using an everyday
weapon?"

"So what does it do?" asked Max.

"These little beauties are called Z-Bots," Krusher informed Max. "And their favorite pastime is playing with human brains. They particularly like CHILDREN'S brains! You see, when the children of your world get their greedy hands on these, I will switch on the Activation Pod. Then each and every child will fall under my control."

"You're not serious, are you?" said Max.

"You'd better believe it," snarled Krusher. "They will be my army of mindless and willing slaves—ready to take over the world! And seeing as you're so interested in how the Z-Bots work, I think it's time for a trial run— OOOOWWWW!"

At that moment, Max stamped hard on Krusher's foot.

Krusher released Max from his grip. Max sprinted toward a narrow gap between two of the shelving units and squeezed into it.

"FIND THAT HUMAN CHILD!" Krusher screamed.

Max peered out from behind the shelves. A couple of drones were loading crates into the last of the trucks.

I have to follow that truck!

Max edged out a fraction. But just as he was about to make a run for it, he felt a tug at his leg. He looked down.

It was Metal Meathead.

Max put a finger to his lips. "Good boy," he whispered, "I'm your friend."

Unfortunately, Meathead's affections couldn't be won that easily. He started gnawing at Max's trousers.

"Get off!" hissed Max, desperately trying to escape. But the savage robodog wasn't the only thing he had to worry about. A split second later he heard footsteps quickly approaching.

"GOTCHA!" shouted a triumphant Spike.

"OVER HERE, KRUSHER!"

Spike grabbed Max's arm while Meathead took care of his leg. Together they dragged Max out from behind the unit. Max tried to wriggle free. But he was no match for their combined metallic strength.

Krusher marched over with the Z-Bot. He tossed it to Spike. Spike held it up in front of Max's face. Krusher then whipped out the Activation Pod and pressed the silver button. The pod split in half, and an antenna extended. Krusher pressed another button. The toy robot's eyes began to glow amber.

Max gazed into the robot's eyes, transfixed.

"Relax," came the voice of Krusher. It sounded muffled and echoey.

Max felt a dull sensation in his head. His limbs grew heavy. He slumped forwards.

I'm being hypnotized!

Max had spent years watching magicians who specialized in mind manipulations. He was aware that in a matter of seconds he'd be totally under the Z-Bot's spell.

He focused his brain. He started repeating the mantra "Stop the brain flow, stop the brain flow—"

"JUMP!" commanded Krusher.

He tried to resist. But Max found himself springing up and down.

"Stop the brain flow, stop the brain flow, stop the brain flow."

He continued to jump. But he kept on repeating this. He fought to regain control of his mind. Gradually his thoughts came back into focus. He was himself again.

However, Krusher and Spike thought he was totally under their spell. And he was going to play along with their instructions.

"DANCE!" said Krusher.

Max leaped through the air. Then he pirouetted as if he was a fully paid-up member of the world's finest ballet troupe.

"BE A DOG!" ordered Spike.

Max got onto all fours. He started panting. He barked at Metal Meathead, who growled back fiercely.

"EXCELLENT!" laughed

Krusher. He pressed a sequence of buttons on the Activation Pod. "Our victims will do exactly what we tell them to do!" He turned back to Max. "Now sleep."

Max stood rooted to the spot. A glazed, vacant look spread over his face.

"Right, Meathead," said Krusher. "We have deliveries to supervise. We'll return for you shortly."

Meathead drooled.

"As for the human," said Krusher dismissively, "you have one simple task."

Meathead looked up eagerly.

"Finish him off!" hissed Krusher.

CHAPTER 18

Krusher and Spike hurried across the
warehouse. They jumped on a motorbike and
sped off. Max was surprised to see they hadn't
bothered with their disguises.

As soon as they'd gone, he snapped out of
his pretend trance. He eyed the dog.

"I guess it's just you and me now, Meathead
old boy," said Max nervously. The robodog
tugged at his trouser leg.

"Look," said Max, "I know we got off to a bad
start. But I'm sure we can work this out."

Metal Meathead shook his head.

"Come on, Meathead!" said Max to the evil robodog. "I can get you a far tastier meal than me! I'll find you some nice juicy bolts. How about it?"

Meathead started barking furiously.

In a lightningquick move, Max kicked out. He sent Meathead flying across the warehouse floor.

Meathead picked himself up. He prepared to lunge at Max again.

I can't keep this up forever!

So Max took the only other option. He ran.

With Metal Meathead in close pursuit, he sprinted towards the nearest shelving unit. He swerved round a corner and found himself in another aisle. He upped his pace. He put a tiny bit more distance between himself and the metal mutt. His mind worked furiously on how to escape Meathead's snapping jaws. He groaned as he reached the end of the aisle.

It was a dead end.

There was nowhere else to run. And he didn't fancy his chances in another one-on-one battle with the savage metal canine.

Then he spotted a gap between the shelving unit and the wall. He squeezed sideways into the space as Metal Meathead tore down the aisle toward him.

Max tugged at the shelving unit.

It didn't budge. He tried again, more forcefully. This time it moved. The unit wobbled for a second and fell toward the floor. Metal Meathead froze as he saw the unit looming over him. Then he yelped and frantically tried to backtrack.

But he was too late.

The unit smashed down on top of the robodog. Max heard a loud crunch as the robodog was squashed flat.

Max had no time to dwell on Metal Meathead's demise. He had a far more vital mission. He ran back into the main section of the warehouse, where the last truck was parked. Its rear door was still open.

Max ran toward the truck and dived into the back. He got in a split second before a drone appeared to slam down the door.

Phew! I don't think he saw me. But he will when he empties out the crates!

Then Max had an idea. He turned to the nearest crate. He pried off the lid.

The crate was packed with Z-Bots. Max pulled them out. He stuffed them behind the pile of crates at the back of the truck. When only a few Z-Bots remained, he climbed into the crate. He piled the Z-Bots on top of himself so that he'd be hidden when the crate was opened. He pulled the lid firmly shut.

It was a bumpy ride. But Max was too busy thinking to notice.

OK, so they have thousands of these Z-Bots. They're going to use them to hypnotize children and turn them into an army. But how are they going to get them into the children's hands? And aren't people going to be suspicious if they see a load of robots running around London?

A short while later the truck stopped. Max heard the voice of Krusher.

"This is the last delivery," he said. "I hope everything is in order."

The truck's rear shutter opened. Max felt his crate being lifted up in the air.

"Weird!" he heard Spike say. "This one feels much heavier than the others!"

Max held his breath. He worried that Spike might open the crate.

"Just get on with it!" Krusher shouted.

Max slid around inside the crate as it was

carried up some steps. He could hear excited cheering and clapping in the distance. Finally, his crate was plonked down.

"Could you just sign for these?" he heard Krusher ask.

"Of course!" giggled a female voice. "You do look fetching in that outfit!"

"Thank you, Madam!" replied Krusher. "It's all part of the service!"

Max prayed his crate wasn't the first to be opened. He was lucky. He heard crates being pried open to gasps of surprise and delight. A couple of minutes went by. Then he heard his crate lid being levered. A beam of light hit his eyes as the Z-Bots above him were taken out of the box.

He came face-to-face with a young woman.

"AAAAARRRRRGGGGHHHH!" she screamed.

MAX FLASH
MISSION 6

CHAPTER 19

"Don't worry!" said Max. He scrambled to his feet. He quickly checked to see if Krusher and Spike were still around. But they'd gone. He stepped out of the crate onto a counter. Then he jumped to the floor.

He was in a shop. The sign said ANDERTONS TOYS.

That's where I'd heard the name Andertons before! This is the biggest toyshop in London.

Outside the shop was a very long and highly excitable line of children.

"I like your outfit," said the shop assistant. She was eyeing Max's warp-proof suit. "Are you part of the promotion, too?"

"Promotion?" asked Max.

She pointed behind him. He turned round and was greeted by the sight of a huge film poster hanging on the wall. It showed Krusher and Spike. The title of the film was Revenge of the Killer Robots.

Max's mouth dropped open.

"This film promotion," she said. "The world premiere is tonight!"

So that's how the robots are managing to avoid suspicion. They're making it seem like they're dressed up as robots as part of the marketing drive for a film.

"And these Z-Bots?" added Max. "They're also part of the marketing?"

"Of course!" The woman laughed. "The company who made the film is giving a free Z-Bot to every kid in the city. That's why all the toy stores are staying open tonight! Isn't it exciting!"

So that's why Krusher and Spike visited those locations all over London. They must have been checking out all of the toyshops and planning their Z-Bot drop-off routes!

"When does the premiere start?" demanded Max urgently.

"At seven o'clock," she answered.

Max looked down at his watch. It was 6:45 P.M.

"Where is it?"

"Leicester Square," she replied.

"You don't have a spare ticket, do you?"

Max gulped. Krusher had said something about "the square." But he didn't mean a square shape. He meant Leicester Square! In twenty-five minutes every kid in London would have their own Z-Bot. All Krusher needed to do then was activate the machines with his Pod. The machines would hypnotize his huge army of children. And he would get the hypnotized children to carry out his orders against the unsuspecting adults. It wouldn't be long before the whole city was under his evil control.

"I've got to go," he said. "Whatever you do, do NOT give those Z-Bots out."

"Hang on a moment, who are you—" the shop assistant began. But at that second, one of the other store assistants opened the main doors. A huge crowd of children ran into the shop. They were fighting and pushing to get their hands on their free Z-Bots.

Max groaned as he imagined an identical scene taking place at every toyshop in London.

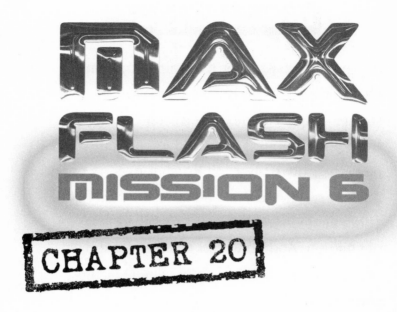

MISSION 6

CHAPTER 20

Max pushed through the crowd of kids.

I'm never going to make it!

He had fifteen . . . no, fourteen minutes before Krusher activated the Z-Bots.

Max noticed a display of mini micro scooters by the shop doors.

"Mind if I borrow this?" he shouted behind him as he grabbed a bright-blue scooter.

Woo hoo!

Pedestrians dived out of the way as Max shot through the automatic shop doors and across

the pavement. He
knew the way to
Leicester Square
because it was
right near the Royal
Theatre where he'd
performed his
magic show.

*But it's much
more fun getting
there this way than
by walking!*

Max reached
Leicester Square at
precisely 6:51 P.M.

I have nine minutes to avert disaster!

Max abandoned the scooter. He weaved
through the throng of children and parents
gathered around the legendary Coronet Cinema.
The cinema was hung with huge banners
advertising Revenge of the Killer Robots.

Max jostled his way through to the front. He saw with panic that every single child was clutching a Z-Bot!

"Hey, watch out!" someone snapped. But Max ignored them and plowed on. He finally reached the front. He craned his neck and saw the red carpet. A horde of photographers were popping flashbulbs.

But there was no sign of Krusher or Spike.

Maybe they're inside already.

Max checked out the guests flashing official invites at the line of security guards.

There's no chance I'll get in that way!

He turned and scanned the rest of the square. That was when he saw them.

High up on the roof of a towering building on the other side of the square were Krusher and Spike. Max could see the Activation Pod in Krusher's hands. Time was running out.

Max fought his way back through the crowd. He scrambled across the square to the tall building. He got closer and saw that the front doors were firmly shut. There were no entry points. He didn't have the right tools to break in.

He'd have to do things a different way.

Max quickly pulled out the Suction Creepers. He took one in each hand. He slammed them as hard as he could against the wall of the building. They made a loud sucking noise as they attached themselves to the brickwork.

Max moved one hand above the other to rapidly scale the wall. He pulled himself up onto the flat roof and ducked behind a chimney.

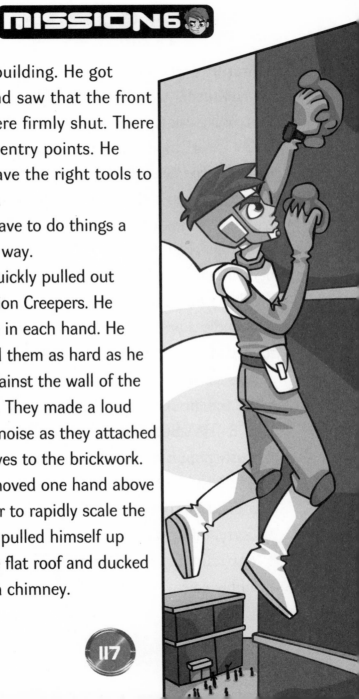

Krusher and Spike were about thirty meters away. Krusher was fiddling with the Activation Pod. Spike was speaking into a mobile phone.

"All is set!" Spike announced to Krusher with delight. "The last Z-Bots will be in children's hands at seven o'clock on the dot—just as we planned. All systems are GO!"

Max checked his watch: 6:55 P.M. He felt panic rising in his chest. He had to stop Krusher from turning thousands of kids into his mindless army! He scurried along the roof towards the robots. But when he was ten meters away, he tripped on an air vent and fell to the ground with a thud.

"IT'S THAT BOY AGAIN!" yelled Spike.

Krusher spun round. His eyes fell on Max. "YOU!" he bellowed. "I thought Metal Meathead finished you off!"

"Sorry, other way round," replied Max.

"Not . . . not . . . my Meathead," said Spike in a wobbly voice.

"Stop blubbing!" snapped Krusher. "And as for you," he said, turning to Max, "you're too late, FOOL. Very soon we will be inviting all of our friends over here to enjoy OUR RULE! Finally we'll have our revenge on the human race for mistreating robots and using us as their slaves!"

"That's RUBBISH!" shouted Max. "We use robots for science and research. Most of them are treated really well! Anyway, what about you and your drones? Aren't they slaves?"

"What about them?" screamed Krusher.

Suddenly a huge spotlight swept over the rooftop. It fixed itself on Max and the robots. There was a gasp from the heaving crowd outside the Coronet. Seconds later everyone started rushing in the direction of the rooftop for a better view of the unfolding events.

"What a fantastic stunt!" someone shouted.

"Can you believe they've planned this for us!" another cried.

"This is better than any film!" hollered another.

Max cursed.

They all think it's part of the show!

Max lunged at the Activation Pod, but Krusher deftly leaped aside. Max fell to the ground.

"OOOOOOH!" gasped the crowd below.

Max struggled to his feet.

"YOU CAN'T DO THIS!" he shouted.

"WE CAN AND WE WILL!" cackled Krusher.

Max prepared to make another lunge at Krusher, but Spike pulled out a large silver laser gun.

"SENSATIONAL!" cheered the crowd.

Max launched himself forward as Spike pressed the trigger.

Max moved like lightning and dived to his left as a red laser bolt shot out of the gun. The bolt flashed past Max. It hit a section of chimney behind him and ricocheted straight back.

"AWESOME!" shouted the crowd.

Spike was directly in the line of fire.

The bolt caught Spike full on the chest and sent him flying backward. He smashed straight into Krusher. They tumbled toward the edge of the roof.

Spike threw out his hand as he fell and grabbed Max by the ankles.

Together, all three of them toppled right over the edge of the roof.

MISSION 6

CHAPTER 21

"NOOOOOOOOO!" they screamed in unison as they plummeted through the air.

They hurtled downward. But Max spotted a large striped awning at the front of a restaurant below. Whether it would be strong enough to break their fall was another matter.

They all hit its springy surface and bounced high up into the air.

Max saw his chance. He shot upward and lashed out with his left leg. He booted Spike right in the middle of his metal stomach.

The robot screamed and went flying over the edge of the awning. He landed on the cobblestones with an almighty crash. He smashed into a thousand pieces. The crowd gasped and edged backwards to escape the shards of flying metal.

Max hit the awning a second time and bounced up again. The crowd held its breath as a huge metal fist came smashing toward his face. Max twisted his body into a somersault. He missed the punch and sent the robot shooting forward.

Krusher howled as he plunged off the awning. He hit the ground with tremendous force and shattered into bits.

Max bounced a few more times. Then he came to a stop. He leaned over the side of the awning and spotted the Activation Pod among a huge mess of metal fragments.

He was about to give a sigh of relief. But then he spotted Krusher's disembodied hand out of the corner of his eye. It was scuttling over the cobbles toward the Activation Pod.

Max leaped off the awning toward the Pod. He rolled over on the ground to break his fall. He scrambled to his feet.

But the hand had got there first. A long metal finger extended and hovered over the silver button.

Max dived forward. He kicked the Pod out of the hand's reach. There was a sickening CRUNCH as he brought his right foot down on the hand with all his might.

Good riddance!

Max bent down and picked up the Activation Pod.

There was an outbreak of thunderous applause from the watching crowd. They were

standing some way back by now. Max looked up at the kids with their Z-Bots. They were not hypnotized. They were not an army. Max had foiled the robots' Great Plan!

But the screeching of tires suddenly diverted his attention. A black van skidded to a halt a few meters away from him. Two figures wearing ski masks leaped out.

More robots! No way!

Max began to run right away. But one of them seized him by the shoulder and threw him into the back of the van. The door slammed shut. He heard the lock click. He tried the handle, but it wouldn't budge. He was trapped. He looked out through a glass panel in the door as the two figures switched on a large, black vacuum-cleaner type object. The object started sucking up all of the metal fragments.

The crowd burst into applause again. These film-marketing people had thought of everything. They even had a speedy cleanup operation!

At least Max still had the Activation Pod.

Max thought fast. If these two got hold of it, they'd be able to activate the Z-Bots. Then all of his work would be for nothing! He didn't want to try smashing the Pod in case he activated the Z-Bots by accident. So he tucked it under his warp-proof suit in desperation.

The van door was yanked open. Two huge sacks of metal fragments were tossed into the back. The doors were then slammed shut again. The engine sprang to life, and the van sped out of the square.

Max's body tensed up. Surely it wouldn't be long before they tried to pry the Pod off him? How was he going to get out of this one? Then the van came to a sudden stop. The panel separating the cab from the back slid open. The two figures whispered something to each other. Then they slowly peeled off their ski masks.

Max was astonished. They weren't robots at all. It was his mom and dad.

MISSION 6

CHAPTER 22

"What the . . . ?" gulped Max in utter
amazement. He crawled over to them.

Mom reached her arms through the gap
and gave him a massive hug. "Sorry about the
kidnapping," she said. "Hope you weren't too
freaked out?"

"I'm fine," replied Max. "But what are you
two doing here?"

"Zavonne's team have been monitoring
the warehouse. They tracked you to Leicester
Square," explained Dad.

"They realized there might be some sort of face-off," added Mom. "We were just round the corner at the theater. So Zavonne sent us in."

"You did brilliantly back there," grinned Dad. "You stopped them just in time."

"Absolutely!" Mom beamed. "Fantastic work!"

"Hang on a sec," said Max. "I thought you two gave up on DFEA stuff years ago."

"So did we." Mom grinned. "But we were hardly going to refuse a job that involved helping our own son out, were we!"

A massive battle with power-crazed robots. A lift home from your parents at the end of the day. Could life get any crazier?

"Max," said another voice.

Max turned round and saw the familiar face of Zavonne projected onto the wall of the van.

"A courier will be visiting your home in one hour to collect the Activation Pod and what remains of the robots."

"OK," replied Max.

"I take it you used all three gadgets?"

"I did," said Max.

Zavonne pursed her lips.

Come on, Zavonne. Praise me for once! I saved the world's kids from turning into evil earth-wreckers! Instead they've all just got free Z-Bots to play with!

"The portal in the warehouse leading from our world to theirs has been permanently shut down by our operatives," said Zavonne. "And the warehouse was burned down in an 'unfortunate' industrial fire. So no evidence of anything untoward is left."

"He did well, didn't he?" called Mom from the front of the van.

Zavonne paused. Max held his breath.

"The mission is now complete," said Zavonne flatly.

But as her face disappeared from the screen, Max thought he caught her giving him a wink.

"After all your heroics, do you fancy a day out tomorrow?" asked Mom.

"Definitely!" replied Max.

"We could catch a film," said Dad. "How do you fancy Revenge of the Killer Robots?"

Max groaned. His mom and dad started laughing, and the van sped on into the night.

EPILOGUE

Krusher's voice could be heard in a maximum-security DFEA strong room talking to Spike.

"You see that piece over there?"

"Yes."

"That's one of my fingers."

"No it isn't," replied Spike. "It's one of mine!"

"I can recognize my own finger!" insisted Krusher.

"It's not yours," sulked Spike.

Their disembodied mouths scowled at each other. Their mouths were surrounded by thousands and thousands of their body parts.

"I guess rebuilding ourselves might take a while, then," said Spike quietly.

"If we're lucky," replied Krusher sourly.

They were silent for a few seconds more.

"Krusher?" said Spike.

"Yes."

"I've got this itch on my left ear."

"So?"

"You couldn't scratch it with that bit of your jaw could you?"

"No way!"

"Go on."

"No."

"Please?"

Krusher sighed heavily. "All right," he said reluctantly. He gave Spike's ear a quick

scratch. "But don't tell anybody."

"Of course not," promised Spike.

"Is that better?"

"Yeah, thanks."

They were silent for another few seconds.

"Hey, Krusher?"

"What is it this time?"

"It's the bottom of my right nostril. You couldn't just . . . ?"

"Forget it," snapped Krusher.

Have you got the rest of my books?

MAX FLASH
MISSION 2
SUPERSONIC

Jonny Zucker
Illustrated by Ned Woodman

GOT IT ?

Jonny Zucker
Illustrated by Ned Woodman

GOT
IT ?

GOT
IT ?

Jonny Zucker
Illustrated by Ned Woodman

GOT
IT ?